Dog Applause

Let's Hear It For

Golden Retrievers

Written by

Piper Welsh

Rourke
Educational Media

rourkeeducationalmedia.com

Scan for Related Titles
and Teacher Resources

www.rourkeeducationalmedia.com

PHOTO CREDITS: Cover, © Vendula Plackova; Page 4: © raywoo; Page 5, 14: © Jens Stolt; Page 6: © Eric Is-selée (Weimaraner, Chocolate Labrador), © Willeecole (Cocker Spaniel); Page 7: © Boris Djuranovic; Page 8: © anirav (Golden Retriever), © Erik Lam (Yellow Labrador); Page 9: © David Acosta Allely; Page 10, 16: © Vendula Plackova; Page 12: © Erik Lam (Irish Setter, Bloodhound), © Eric Isselée (Black Labrador); Page 13: © Sunheyy; Page 15: © Lynn M. Stone; Page 17, 19: © Martin Valigursky; Page 18: © Julija Sapic; Page 20: © Moori; Page 21: © Godrick; Page 22: © Isselee

Edited by: Precious McKenzie

Cover design by: Renee Brady
Interior design by: Ashley Morgan

Library of Congress PCN Data

Welsh, Piper.
  Let's Hear It For Golden Retrievers / Piper Welsh.
    p. cm. -- (Dog Applause)
  Includes index.
  ISBN 978-1-62169-864-7 (hardcover)
  ISBN 978-1-62169-759-6 (softcover)
  ISBN 978-1-62169-965-1 (e-Book)
Library of Congress Control Number: 2013936475

Also Available as:

Rourke Educational Media
Printed in the United States of America,
North Mankato, Minnesota

Rourke
Educational Media

rourkeeducationalmedia.com

customerservice@rourkeeducationalmedia.com • PO Box 643328 Vero Beach, Florida 32964

Table of Contents

Golden Retrievers.................................5

Look at Me!....................................8

History of the Golden Retriever...............11

A Popular Breed.............................17

A Loyal Companion 18

Doggie Advice 22

Glossary 23

Index.....................................24

Websites to Visit 24

Show What You Know 24

Golden Retrievers

Long ago someone said that the dog was "man's best friend." Now, people say, the Golden Retriever is everyone's best friend! Perhaps no breed of dog shows more **affection** toward people than the handsome, tail-wagging Golden Retriever.

Golden Retriever Facts

Weight:	55-75 pounds (25-34 kilograms)
Height:	21.5-24 inches (54-61 centimeters)
Country of Origin:	Great Britain
Life Span:	12-13 years

Like other retriever breeds, the Golden loves to fetch, or retrieve. The love of retrieving is part of the Golden's **instinct**.

Weimaraner

Chocolate Labrador

Cocker Spaniel

There are many other dog breeds in the sporting group.

As a service dog, the Golden Retriever wants to please their master because of their caring and compassionate personailty.

Goldens are one of the so-called sporting, or gundog, breeds. Goldens are trained by hunters to retrieve ducks, geese, and other game birds. Goldens are also one of the three breeds commonly used as service dogs.

Look at Me!

Goldens have fine, athletic builds similar to those of other retrievers. A **well-bred** Golden has a broad head with wide, floppy ears and a fairly square **muzzle**.

Long hair helps separate Goldens from yellow Labrador Retrievers. Goldens wear a fringe of hair, called feathers, along their legs, underside, and tail.

The coats of Golden Retrievers range from red-gold to nearly white. A dense undercoat lies beneath the long outer coat.

Golden Retriever

Labrador Retriever

Can you name some of the differences between a Golden Retriever and a yellow Labrador Retriever?

Golden Retrievers can be trusted to find something to play fetch with anywhere they are taken.

Even today, many Goldens are trained to help hunt fowl.

History of the Golden Retriever

Lord Tweedmouth was a wealthy Scotsman. He loved hunting and he loved hunting dogs. The common retrievers of Tweedmouth's day had dark, flat coats. Tweedmouth wanted a handsome retriever with a longhaired, yellow coat.

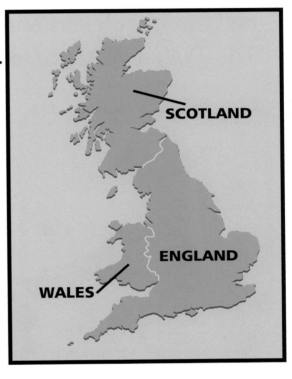

In 1868, Tweedmouth **mated** a male yellow retriever with a female Tweed Water Spaniel. Their four pups weren't Golden Retrievers. They were, however, the beginning of the breed.

Over the next several years, Tweedmouth used the grown pups and several other dogs as parents. He used Red Setters, a Bloodhound, and more retrievers and Tweed Water Spaniels. The Tweed Water Spaniel is now **extinct**.

Irish Setter

Bloodhound

Black Labrador Retriever

Golden Retrievers get their characteristics from several different breeds.

Golden Retrievers were first shown in England in 1908.

Many people considered Tweedmouth's dogs just a yellow variety of the Flat-Coated Retriever. But in 1912, The Kennel Club of England recognized the Golden Retriever as a breed.

Lord Tweedmouth's sons had brought Goldens to America by 1900. Still, the American Kennel Club (AKC) did not accept Goldens as a separate breed until 1925.

Did You Know?

Golden Retrievers have acted in many movies and television shows such as *Air Bud, Homeward Bound,* and *Full House.*

In the early 1900s, darker Golden Retriever coats were favored over the lighter variety.

The Golden Retriever is considered a family dog because of its loyalty and gentle nature.

A Popular Breed

The great majority of Golden Retrievers are not working dogs. They are household companions. Their friendly nature makes them especially popular in homes with small children.

Golden Retrievers are one of the most loved breeds in the United States. The American Kennel Club ranked the Golden Retriever as the third most popular **purebred** in the nation for 2012.

A Loyal Companion

Almost always good-natured, Goldens demand human attention. A Golden Retriever begins wagging its tail each time a stranger appears. A Golden seems to welcome everyone as a new friend.

Because of their loyal nature, Goldens make good watch dogs and will bark whenever they sense danger.

Goldens also love to swim and play in the water.

Generally, adult Goldens are calm, relaxed dogs that bark very little. But they are athletic dogs with plenty of energy. They love to swim, run, romp, play fetch, and sniff about the woods.

Each breed of dog has certain standards. Standards include such things as proper height, weight, color, and shape. Many Goldens are entered in shows that judge how closely they meet the breed standards.

Goldens are eager, easy learners. They love to please their human masters. They do very well in **obedience** tests where they follow a variety of commands. Most Golden Retriever owners agree, there is nothing better than this breed.

Goldens are skilled at competing in events such as dock jumping and field trials.

Doggie Advice

Puppies are cute and cuddly, but buying one should never be done without serious thought. Choosing the right breed of dog requires some homework. And remember that a dog will require more than love and great patience. It will require food, exercise, grooming, a warm, safe place to live, and medical care.

A dog can be your best friend, but you need to be its best friend, too. For more information about buying and owning a dog, contact the American Kennel Club at *www.akc.org/index.cfm* or the Canadian Kennel Club at *www.ckc.ca*.

Glossary

affection (uh-FEK-shun): friendliness toward another creature

extinct (iks-TINKT): to have gone out of existence

instinct (IN-stinkt): action or behavior with which an animal is born, rather than learned behavior

mated (MAY-tud): to have been paired with another dog for the purpose of having pups

muzzle (MUZ-uhl): the nose and jaws of an animal; the snout

obedience (oh-BEE-dee-ehns): the willingness to follow someone's direction or command

purebred (PYOOR-bred): an animal of a single (pure) breed

well-bred (WEL-BRED): to have come from outstanding ancestors and parents

Index

breeds   6, 7, 17

coat(s)   8, 11

Flat-Coated Retriever   13

hair   8

instinct   6

Labrador Retriever(s)   8

obedience tests   20

purebred   17

standards   20

Tweed Water Spaniel(s)   11, 12

Tweedmouth, Lord   11, 12, 14

Websites to Visit

www.akc.org/breeds/golden_retriever

www.dogbreedinfo.com/goldenretriever.htm

www.grca.org

Show What You Know

1. What are some of the Golden Retrievers' favorite activities?
2. Besides being a pet, what other things are Golden Retrievers used for?
3. What is the country of origin of the Golden Retriever?